The AMAZING COLLECTION of JOEY CORNELL

by Candace Fleming

illustrated by Gérard DuBois

schwartz & wade books · new york

Joey Cornell collected—

everything . . .

anything . . .

that sparked his imagination or delighted his eye.

"If I like it, I keep it," Joey always said.

At first, he stowed his collection in his bedroom.

But it grew . . .

and grew . . .

and grew, until . . .

Joey gathered it together, packed it up
and moved it all out to the barn.

His sisters made fun of him.

"Trash picker," said Betty.

"Pack rat," said Helen.

"Weird," said their mother, "but wonderful."

Whenever Mrs. Cornell shopped in the city,

she searched for objects to enchant her son—

a silver charm,

a cork ball,

a soap bubble pipe.

"What will you do with them?" she asked.

Joey shrugged. "Who knows?"

He added them to his collection.

Joey's father brought home treasures, too.

Like a magician, he pulled them from coat sleeves and vest pockets—

odd-shaped pebbles,

butterfly wings,

sheet music to long-forgotten songs.

Joey added these to his collection, too.

By the time Joey was eight,

his collection looked like this:

That same year, his father brought home

two tickets to see . . .

HARRY HOUDINI!

Tied with chains.

Locked in an iron box.

Joey sat spellbound.

Days later, in the junkyard, he spied a rusty iron safe.

His scalp tingled, and goose bumps rose on his arms.

"Magical," he whispered.

He dragged it home.

"What do you want *that* for?" asked Betty.

Joey shrugged. "Who knows?"

He added it to his collection.

By the time Joey was nine, his collection

looked like this:

That year, an old lady and her parrot moved into the neighborhood.

Time and again, Joey gazed at the bird.

One day, a single feather drifted out of the cage and into his hand.

He heard the rustling of palm trees.

He tasted sea salt on his lips.

"Exotic," he whispered.

"What will you do with *that*?" asked Helen.

"Who knows?" Joey said.

He carried the feather home and added it to his collection.

By the time he was eleven, Joey's collection looked like this:

That year Joey discovered the universe.

Sitting on the front steps, he peered into the night sky and made up stories about the stars for his sisters. . . .

"Once upon a time, a ballerina danced on the head of a comet."

Wandering, he spotted a battered telescope in a secondhand store.

When he squinted into it, he saw—

Moonbeams and flare stars.

Galaxies spinning in the darkness.

"Heavenly," he whispered.

He carted the telescope home.

"Why do you want *that*?" asked Robert.

"Who knows?" said Joey.

He added it to his collection.

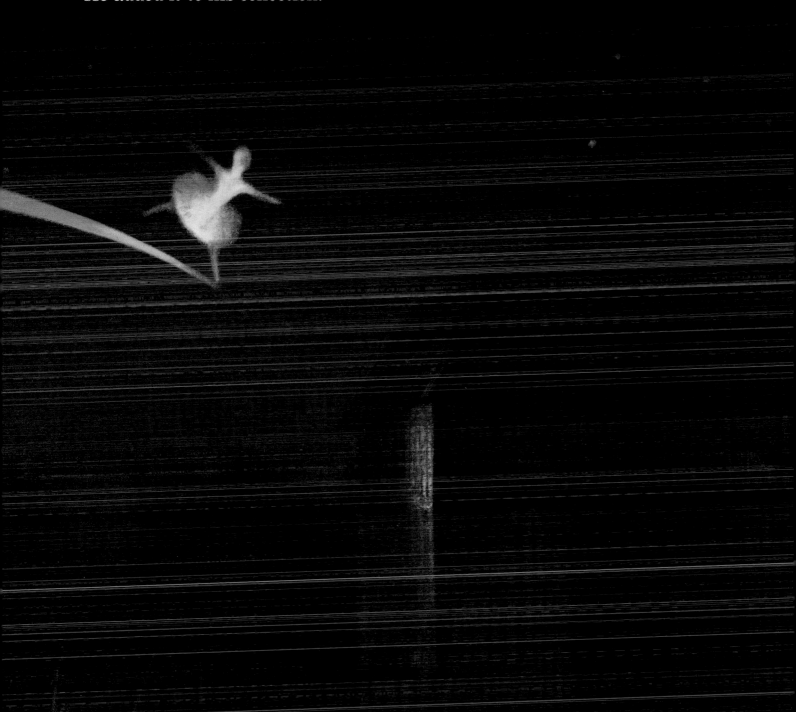

By the time he was thirteen, his collection looked like this:

That year, his father grew pale and weak. He stopped going to work.

He stopped getting out of bed.

It was still dark the morning Joey awoke to the sound of hurrying feet and harsh coughing. He looked out his window just as his father was being rushed into an ambulance.

Joey never saw his father again.

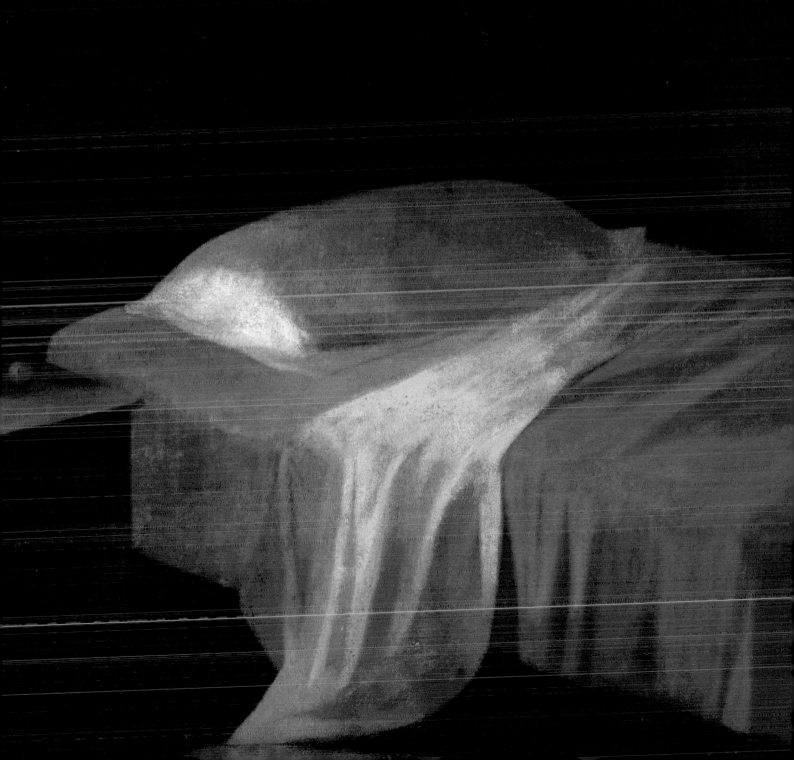

Now the house felt cold and empty.

And Joey lost himself in his collection—sifting, layering, mixing, making.

Oh, how he wished his family could feel happy, just for one afternoon.

He looked down at what he'd done.

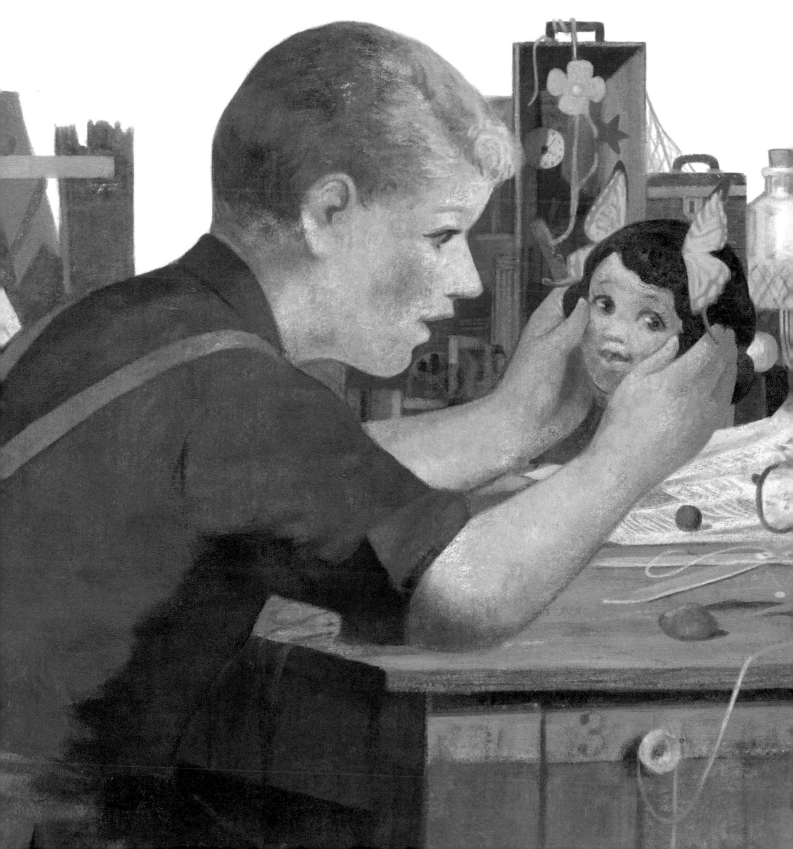

A doll's head sprouting butterfly wings?

Sheet music puffing from a soap bubble pipe?

Joey shook his head in wonder. The objects looked as if they

had *always* belonged to one another. They looked *right* together.

They looked like . . .

"Art," he whispered.

An idea sparked.

Joey got to work.

Days later, Joey handed out tickets
to his family.

When they opened the barn door,
they were astonished.

Dozens of ordinary objects had been

assembled,

assorted,

arranged

in a way that made them—

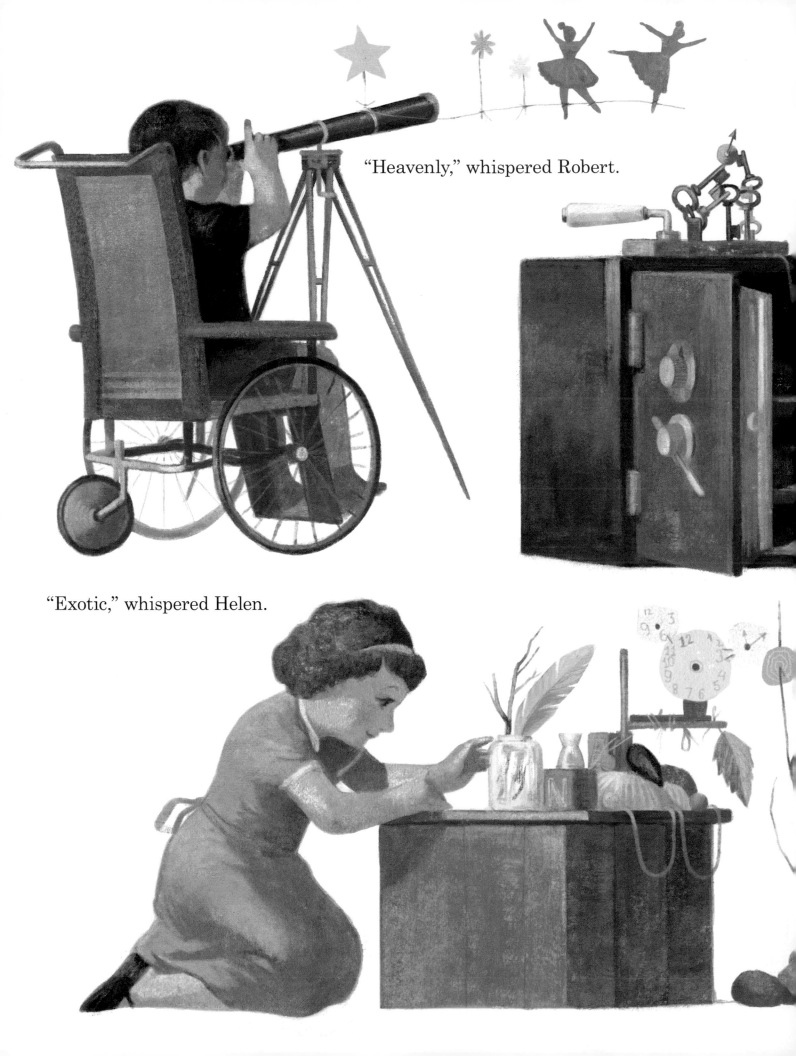

"Heavenly," whispered Robert.

"Exotic," whispered Helen.

"Magical," whispered Betty.

"And wonderful!" added
their mother. She wrapped
Joey in a hug.

Then they all looked at Joey's amazing collection again . . .

and again . . .

and even again.

It was dark before they left.

That was when Joey noticed a ticket lying on the ground.

He picked it up.

"If I like it, I keep it," he said.

And he added it to his collection.

AUTHOR'S NOTE

This story is about a boy who never stopped collecting. By the time Joseph Cornell was a grown-up, living in Flushing, New York, with his aging mother and his brother, Robert (who had cerebral palsy), his collection looked like the photograph below left.

Some objects had even followed him from childhood, including an iron safe, a battered telescope, and a handmade ticket admitting its bearer to his "Relic Museum," all of which appear in this story. In later years, Joseph would call his collection "a diary journal, picture gallery, museum, and clearing house for dreams and visions."

As an artist, Joseph became famous for putting various objects into small wooden boxes, carefully choosing things that connected with his passions, obsessions, and memories. "Who knows what those objects will say to each other?" he once remarked.

Joseph's first art show really did take place in the family's barn—in Nyack, New York, in 1917. Meant to cheer up his family after his father's death from a blood disease that same year, the exhibit featured a loaf of bread chained inside an iron safe, among other displays.

Joseph's last art show was held fifty-five years later at the Cooper Union school in New York City. Because it was meant for "Children Only," he hung his boxes about four feet off the floor and was one of the few grown-ups present. Young people, he always claimed, understood his work best because their vivid imaginations allowed them to *see* the magic.

Shelves from the grown-up artist's collection, c. 1960 (Terry Shutté)

Cornell at Cooper Union, 1972 (Denise Hare)

"I never had an art lesson," Joseph said. "I can't draw, paint, [or] sculpt." And yet he became one of the most influential American artists of the twentieth century. "The question," he said, "is not what you look at, but what you see."

SELECTED BIBLIOGRAPHY

Ashton, Dore. *A Joseph Cornell Album*. New York: Da Capo Press, 2002.

Edwards, Jason, and Stephanie L. Taylor, eds. *Joseph Cornell: Opening the Box*. Oxford, England: Peter Lang, 2003.

McShine, Kynaston, ed. *Joseph Cornell*. Munich, Germany: Prestal Verlag in cooperation with the Museum of Modern Art, New York, 1990.

NOTES

"Relic Museum": McShine, 93.

"diary journal, picture gallery . . .": http://americanart.si.edu/education/insights /cappy/13acornellbio.html.

"Who knows what . . .": Edwards and Taylor, 244.

"Children Only": Ashton, 224.

"see": ibid.

"I never had an art . . .": Ashton, 4.

"The question is not . . .": http://americanart.si.edu/education/insights /cappy/13acornellbio.html.

Cassiopeia #1, 1960 (Art @ The Joseph and Robert Cornell Memorial Foundation/Licensed by VAGA, New York, NY)

The Hotel Eden, 1945 (Art @ The Joseph and Robert Cornell Memorial Foundation/Licensed by VAGA, New York, NY)

Soap Bubble Set, 1948 (Art @ The Joseph and Robert Cornell Memorial Foundation/Licensed by VAGA, New York, NY)

To Tristan
—C.F.

To the dreamers who showed me there was a way
—G.D.

Text copyright © 2018 by Candace Fleming
Jacket and interior illustrations copyright © 2018 by Gérard DuBois

All rights reserved. Published in the United States by Schwartz & Wade Books, an imprint of Random House Children's Books,
a division of Penguin Random House LLC, New York.

Schwartz & Wade Books and the colophon are trademarks of Penguin Random House LLC.

Visit us on the Web! rhcbooks.com

Educators and librarians, for a variety of teaching tools, visit us at RHTeachersLibrarians.com

Library of Congress Cataloging-in-Publication Data
Names: Fleming, Candace, author. | DuBois, Gérard, illustrator.
Title: The amazing collection of Joey Cornell / by Candace Fleming ; illustrated by Gérard DuBois.
Description: First edition. | New York : Schwartz & Wade Books, 2018. | Audience: Ages 4–8. | Audience: K to Grade 3.
Identifiers: LCCN 2017006761 | ISBN 978-0-399-55238-0 (hardcover) | ISBN 978-0-399-55239-7 (library binding)
ISBN 978-0-399-55240-3 (ebook)
Subjects: LCSH: Cornell, Joseph—Juvenile literature.
Classification: LCC N6537.C66 F59 2018 | DDC 700.92—dc23

The text of this book is set in Century Schoolbook.
The illustrations were rendered in acrylic on paper and digital
Book design by Rachael Cole

MANUFACTURED IN CHINA
2 4 6 8 10 9 7 5 3 1
First Edition